The Adventures of Brisky Bear & Trooper Dog
Be Kind, Be Friendly, Be Thankful

Created by Steve Bolt
Written by Phil Callaway
Illustrated by Sharon Dahl

Glory Be Collectibles
www.glorybe.com

Dedicated To Friends Everywhere

This Book
Presented To:

_____

By:

_____

Trooper Dog and Brisky Bear were best friends. They loved to eat pizza.

They loved to swim at the old swimming hole. When Brisky Bear wanted honey, Trooper Dog found it for him—and snapped at bees. When Trooper Dog couldn't find a flea, Brisky Bear found it—and scratched his back.

Brisky Bear was going to leave on a big trip. On the night before he left, they sat by their favorite spot roasting marshmallows and making some-mores.

"Why are you going away?" asked Trooper Dog.

"I'm going to work on a farm," answered Brisky Bear.

"Where?"

"Up the river."

"Can I come?"

"No, you must stay here."

"Will you be gone long?"

"I'll be gone a long time. But you know, you are a hero, Trooper Dog."

"What do you mean, Brisky Bear?"

"I mean you're a hero because there's a lot to take care of around here. You can help others have good attitudes. Be the Dog, old buddy!"

"And you'll be the hero at the farm, Brisky Bear; I just know you will."

"Hey, we're heroes together."

Trooper Dog knew that what Brisky Bear said would be hard on him. He went from sad to mad. He stomped and he stamped. He fumed and he fussed. Brisky Bear scratched words on a piece of bark. It said, *"Trooper Dog and Brisky Bear. Friends for Always."*

"There are three things I want you to do while I'm gone," said Brisky Bear. He lifted Trooper Dog's ear and told him what they were.

On the first day after Brisky Bear left, Trooper Dog was still upset. He wanted Brisky Bear to come back. He sat in his favorite spot, a little gray cloud hanging over him. He hung his head low for awhile but a cool breeze soon blew that old cloud away.

"Hey, maybe things will get better," he thought. "It could be my lucky day!"

Lucky Day

Oh, when I see the sun shining in the sky,
And I watch all the pretty little blue birds fly,
I've got to say, "Hey, today's my lucky day."

When a dark rain cloud shows up overhead,
I see all the happy little flowers in their bed,
And I say, "Hey, today's your lucky day."
No matter how happy or sad I might feel,
I can always find something to make me
    kick up my heels.

There's no situation, there's no circumstance,
That could keep my feet from wishing they could
    get up and dance.
Oh, you might wonder about this spring in my step,
I'm just thinking about fun things I haven't done yet.
Hey, I've got to say, "Everyday's my lucky day."

BE KIND. B.B.

It seemed like the song helped for awhile, but then Trooper Dog kind of got grumpy again with his friends. He sure didn't feel like a hero.

Along came a piece of bark from upstream. It said, *"Be kind."* It was signed BB, and he remembered the first thing Brisky Bear had said.

He stopped snapping at Smudge the cat and bought him tuna pizza. He stopped barking at Sylvester Squirrel and helped him find acorns. And he knew that Brisky Bear was right: If you want to start smiling, be kind.

On the second day Trooper Dog was lonely. He missed eating pizza with Brisky Bear. He grumbled and he mumbled. He sulked and he snuffled. He chased Smudge the cat up the tallest tree. He barked at Sylvester Squirrel. Then he sat in his favorite spot all alone.

Along came a piece of bark from upstream. It said, "*Be friendly. BB.*" And he remembered the second thing Brisky Bear had said.

He stopped barking at Sylvester Squirrel. He told Smudge the cat he was sorry. "Want to play checkers, Smudge?" During the game Smudge told him that singing sometimes can help a lot when you're feeling down.

Just then Ribby the Frog jumped out of the stream and hopped right over to where Trooper Dog and Smudge were playing and sang him this song.

Ribby Dibby Dibby

Oh, when your heart is down, and you look
    around,
Sing a little song like this...
Ribby Dibby Dibby, Rubby Dubby Dubby,
Sing away the blues.

When your world is sad, and you're feeling
    bad,
Tap a little tune like this...
Ribby Dibby Dibby, Rubby Dubby Dubby,
Tap away the blues.
Ribby Dibby Dibby, Rubby Dubby Dubby,
Sing away the blues.

Trooper Dog reached out to thank Ribby and gave him a pat on the head. "Thanks for the song, Ribby." And so Trooper Dog was learning that if you want friends, be friendly.

On the third day Trooper Dog didn't feel so lucky anymore and he started to worry. What if the sky might rain and the day might be sad? He thought about how he looked. His tail was too short and he only had four feet. He moaned and he groaned. He whimpered and he whined.

He told Smudge how bad things were. He told Sylvester Squirrel how sad things were. Then he sat in his favorite spot with a great big frown. He didn't even feel like singing and he sure didn't feel like a hero.

Along came a piece of bark from upstream. It said, "*Be thankful.*" It was signed BB. And he remembered the third thing Brisky Bear had said. He told Ribby again how glad he was for new friends.

He told Sylvester Squirrel about ice cream and bought him his very first cone. And he knew that Brisky Bear was right. If you want to be happy, be thankful. He also knew that heroes have to have good attitudes. He decided right then and there to be the most thankful dog alive!

Yes, he would be a hero just like Brisky Bear.

One day Trooper Dog and his friends sat together at Trooper Dog's favorite spot. They laughed and talked of all the things they were glad about. They even ate cheese pizza with extra tuna.

"I hear something," said Smudge.

"Me too," said Trooper Dog.

"Sounds like singing to me," said Sylvester.

Then something came floating along. It wasn't the bark with "*Be Kind*" on it. It wasn't the bark with "*Be Friendly*" on it. It wasn't the bark with "*Be Thankful*" on it.

No, it was a big old bear floating on a log and singing out in a loud bass voice.

"Look, here comes Brisky Bear!"

"Our hero! Yeah!"

It was BB himself–Brisky Bear–home from upstream, flying his *Friends for Always* flag at the top of his raft and waving and grinning, just ready for a great big old bear hug.

Friends for Always

Takin' a walk, throwin' a ball around,
Hangin' around in the country, or goin' to town,
Or just havin' a talk by the old picket fence,
Everything's better with a friend.

Friends for always, friends forever,
In big and in small ways, for worse or for better.
Havin' a friend means you're never alone,
When a friend's in your heart, you're always at home.

Oh, friends for always, friends forever,
On happy or sad days, whatever the weather.
I'm glad to know that we'll be forever together,
Friends for always.

Sharin' a toy, sharin' a candy bar,
A friend is a hero, whether near or far.
You can always depend, from beginnin' to end,
Everything's better with a friend.